Will You Please Marry Me?

A Fiction Novel

By Analise

MILTON & HUGO L.L.C.
4407 Park Ave., Suite 5
Union City, NJ 07087, USA

Website: *www. miltonandhugo.com*
Hotline: *1- 888-778-0033*
Email: *info@miltonandhugo.com*

Ordering Information:
Quantity sales. Special discounts are granted to corporations, associations, and other organizations. For more information on these discounts, please reach out to the publisher using the contact information provided above.

Library of Congress Control Number: 2024911549
ISBN-13:   979-8-89285-123-7   [Paperback Edition]
                979-8-89285-125-1   [Hardback Edition]
                979-8-89285-124-4   [Digital Edition]

Rev. date: 05/29/2024

To my daughter, Kya Hazel. I hope your actions will be smarter than mine have been.

And to anyone who still has a chance to not blow it with the love of their life.

*Disclaimer: You are reading *Analise's view* of the story. All views are her own as a fallen sinner.

CHAPTER 1

Wednesday, January 3, 2024
*An entry that I planned to read aloud to Dawson the next evening.

Dawson,

You are such a strong man. Good at the core. You need to take better care of yourself and not let frustration take over your brain as often, forgetting how powerful your kindness is paired with your knowledge. You still have so much life ahead of you. My heart can't begin to express to you how sorry I am that our time together did not go the way it could have. And I am sorry for the time I held you back from something better for you, more honoring to God.

What I am about to write down and share is so beyond catastrophic, tragic, sick… It's like a gruesome horror documentary or a soap-opera nightmare. I just ask that you listen and hear my best shot at explaining the answers owed to you.

The complete truth means your world shattering at my hand, yet again—the absolute last thing you deserve.

I have to preface this with, I truly believe that my breast augmentation surgery severely impacted by ability to make some rational decisions or played a small part. It was about that time three years ago when something changed or got worse for me mentally. However, it doesn't come as an excuse for how I have sinned.

I'm ready to free myself from every lie that I have spoken and release you to pursue anything that's left for you.

A big part of me knew we were reaching new heights and wants to keep trying in building the relationship of my dreams with you (which I have tried but failed at so many times before).

But I have built on sand, and it is not possible to keep standing. Every night I lie awake thinking about how I can't lie to you anymore. I see how good you are.

The only way I can prove to myself, and to everyone, that I am not a literal psycho is to tell the truth starting now.

To explain that somehow I have been operating in a criminal scheme and lying for two years (this includes the half a year while pregnant and almost a year and a half of Kya's life).

Everything real with you is now a lie because of one terrible decision.

In October of 2021, when I was devastated after another one of our breakups where I asked if you wanted to marry me and the answer wasn't yes, I made an insane decision to take matters into my own hands in trying to become a mother. I acted as a complete whore, and I went on a hinge date specifically to get pregnant. I had a one-night stand after taking an ovulation test. The man's name as I knew it was Sven. I only knew that he was a white blonde German citizen who was very kind and patient and worked as a bartender instructor.

I found out that I was pregnant shortly after, and I had every intention of raising my baby alone.

I was not acting rationally here, obviously. I had just bought a small townhouse in a nice part of town, thanks to a steady career for a young person, thinking I could raise my baby within miles of both men, without telling anyone what was growing inside of me (until or unless someone came after me).

In fact, I do remember having a few fantasies of being brave, telling you that I was pregnant with another man's baby—and asking if there was any way you wanted life with us still. But instead, the two times I saw you while I knew I was pregnant, we ended up not talking much, if you know what I mean. And then the third time I saw you, I did think it would be the last time I saw you.

I had tried to desperately pour out my admiration for you during those previous two dates, knowing my time with you left was limited and knowing I still wanted to reach my life goal of hearing you say you were infatuated with me too and that you wanted to marry me too.

I knew my stomach was going to start to show soon. (I was almost four months pregnant on this third date.) But I thought it looked like it was just bloating. Just like normal, during this date, you weren't sharing in verbal infatuation for me, just the physical: willingness to take off my clothes.

It's true, I was playing with *fire* when we were still hooking up as I was a few months pregnant.

When you noticed that I was pregnant on that third day, Dawson, while we were making love, I just didn't (at the time) have it in me to tell me you that I had slept with someone else—simply because you would not commit to marriage with me after almost two years of knowing who I am and how much passion I felt for you.

So when you both noticed and assumed the baby was yours, somehow I acted as a sinner, psychopath, split personality, possessed... I don't know. I was too ashamed. I selfishly chose additional time with you by not clarifying the simple reality—she is not your daughter.

Flashback

I gave Dawson a tour of my newly purchased townhome. After we ate our Sunday brunch (pancakes and eggs), we went upstairs. I tried to keep my sweatshirt on, but he took it off halfway through. He noticed a bump and pushed on my stomach so hard that I was scared he might have hurt the baby.

"Are you pregnant? What is that?" he asked.

Panicked, I said, "No, no, I have been eating too much."

Dawson then took a shower. He made me sit there on the sink counter. He stared at me the entire time he was in the shower. (There's never cuddling after sex; he has to rinse).

Dawson got out and said, "Yes, you are."

I had not planned for this topic to come up today, and my flight response was a *stupid* one...really? The whole time he was in the shower, I couldn't have found the right words.

The wild thing was, you would have thought I would have had a plan to clarify the truth. I had already told my sister and parents that

I was pregnant. I had already experienced conversations where they assumed it was Dawson's, and all I said was, "He's going to kill me."

At the time, I thought I'd be in the hospital birthing the baby alone, and that would be a good time to tell them why he wasn't around. Gosh, my dad even tried to convince me to not tell anyone, move in with them, and run away from San Francisco, knowing I wasn't always good at making beneficial decisions for myself.

But now, I imposed *this* situation on myself...I do love Dawson, and he doesn't deserve this, damn it... I may as well have ignited a button clearly labeled "constant internal turmoil and misery" as soon as I decided to let him cling to my pregnant self, saying, "I'll spend the rest of my life making this up to you."

I somehow thought that God would bless our hearts with the miracle of new life. I guess it was nothing more than a desire to be with you, but at the time, I sort of let myself think it was karma for you noticing I was pregnant during a time where all you would commit to was sex. Well, obviously, that was nothing but stupid. Lying allowed Satan to take over my life and step into yours.

Then I completely made most of our first year as parents together miserable, and I account that to the grief I faced, looming doom of the truth. That's probably why I was unable to connect to you fully. I know we had beautiful moments too, but I could not enjoy one minute of the life I had only dreamed of with you: one where you were with me...even though it was by duty and not really choice, and even having your baby wasn't enough to earn the wife title, so that only made the me who was alive at this point even sicker.

I don't know if you're still listening, if you think I belong in a prison or a mental institution for this act. But the only thing I can do to prove that I have *any* true love for you, Dawson, is to tell you now. Let me acknowledge that no sorry cuts it, and I'll give you every penny I can and gladly accept whatever consequences I need to face for betraying you and my honor. I need to prove that I can make decisions in Kya's best interest starting now.

You are a magical man. You have the potential to be a father like your father was. Full of wisdom and strength and power. I'm sorry that I may have failed on God's mission for me thus far, or maybe I accomplished it. I hope to use this story to point Kya to God.

I hope you will father many children of your own to raise up just like you, with a wife you commit to fully, like you never have before.

I'm so sorry. There's a big part of me that would have rather committed suicide over knowing that you know what I did. I hurt you so badly. I would be dead already except that I see now that Kya needs her mommy healthy.

How crazy is it, I even named her with my grandma's name and your grandma's name. Thinking I would have no other option than to kill myself later, I wanted to her name to represent strong legacy.

My plan really was to commit suicide before I rededicated myself to Jesus. No matter how hard this is, I'm going to choose to live through it and turn my life around to die a good person and face God. I already feel better as I write this down, but I have destroyed everything. Moving on and facing the world again with broken souls will be hard for both of us, but it will make us stronger.

I told you and made you think that Kya looks just like me as a baby. But there is no chance your biological kids won't look just like you I know I see Kya's face as the most beautiful, and you see her beauty too, that wild red hair and all. Even though I could see how your family has credibility when they say, no cuteness or intelligence levels can come close to your genes.

You are the most beautiful human to me, Dawson, and I'm sorry for destroying your last few years in certain ways. Is there any chance that you want to remain Kya's legal father, knowing she isn't your blood? Is there any chance we can work through this together?

More likely, you are free to go and punish me like I deserve. Haven't women been stoned and hung for these things? My life choices are only to be blamed on myself. I can't believe I lied every day for two years. I can remember turning bright red, avoiding your baby photos, choking on my words, and walking away from conversations with your parents around who Kya looks like. But somehow, I was able to let Satan control me, for selfish reasons and twisting the true definition of love.

I messed this up bad. I can't fall back on any excuses, as much as I want to name them to help explain myself.

If I hadn't messed this up, if I had been smarter and understood then what I do now about how to treat you and relate to you, we could have had a different life together maybe.

I like to think I would have been a good wife to you, given the opportunity way back a few years ago. But you never know. Maybe my feeling that I will never be the woman to satisfy you is also true, and now you can search for her again. Please don't lose hope in deep, satisfying love like you deserve. I failed, but I know you will give it and receive it so much easier now.

I remember when your friend Winn cheated on Laila, and I cried with her. Or when your mom told me the story about the pastor of your church cheating with his best friend's wife.

These kinds of sexually impure sins shake us to the core. Now I have sinned worse than anyone else. The only good in it is Ms. Kya Hazel, who still has sparkles in her eyes and a whole life to flourish in and meet Jesus herself. Unfortunately, because of my decision, she doesn't have you as a father anymore. I guess she never should have.

I know that you will need lots of time to deliberate with friends and family in how to proceed to destroy me. No one can be on my side after what I have done. I am not even really on my own side. What I have done is wrong. But I hope that one day Kya will forgive me if I start living by the Bible's truth now like never before.

I'm begging you, punish me, but not Kya.

CHAPTER 2

Thursday, January 4, 2024
*Reads journal to him.

I always was a sucker for New Year's resolutions. I decided I couldn't go on another year, much less another day, so I decided to kick over the sandcastle that I accidentally built my life on.

I did not know if I would find the courage, but I hated my life so much that I grabbed the journal off my bed and just went for it without thinking. (I tend to make some decisions like that, I guess.)

Before I told him, he and Kya ate a great dinner together, per normal. He is the reason she eats everything; he convinced her it was cool. I snapped a photo of them cuddling while eating at the dining table, right before the house collapsed—or I kicked it over, rather— even though it appeared to be standing up from the outside.

You'd see storage tubs in the background of that photo I snapped, which I had ordered the night before along with Kya's next size up in clothes, knowing there would be packing going on, not knowing if he would take my baby away from me somehow.

Dawson sighed as I asked if we could talk. *Ugh, another feelings conversation*, he probably thought.

I asked him to come sit next to me on the couch and requested to start recording on his phone before I read the words, proving I was okay with however he wanted to punish me.

At this point, I had gone explosive on Dawson enough times at 10:00 p.m. that he was staying at his house, even though he came over to see Kya after work most days.

By explosive, I mean, I pushed him away by begging for him to marry me (knowing it was a no even after I got pregnant) and then shutting down. Not a great way to love someone, *especially* not if you're lying to them about something fundamental. Nonetheless, I was a miserable, confused liar, and it hurt even worse when things were good between us.

As much as I didn't want to give up on my goal of becoming his wife, that's exactly it. I realized I was wrong for setting my only life goal on hearing him say he wanted to marry me too. I was done with myself on so many levels. Done lying to him and his family. Done fantasizing about running away from my baby. Done trying to make up for my sin instead of confronting it. The only possible solution was acceptance of exile and consequences after telling the truth.

CHAPTER 3

Friday, January 5, 2024
(One day later)

I did it. I read the journal entry to Dawson after we put Kya to sleep last night. Is this real? I have not eaten in days. I puked as soon as I woke up.

As sad as I am, I feel better than I have in a long time. The wreckage is messy. Both processing of deep pain and the unknown loom around me.

I told Dawson the truth. But I'm afraid that getting truly healthy again will not be easy for me. At least, I feel God here with me now, I think.

I never imagined that the first words out of his mouth (after about two minutes of silence), would be, "The Lord is here to forgive you, Analise." I never imaged that his response would be *mercy*.

I thought he would shoot me or kick me for sure. He had a gun on him. So if that doesn't say something about the people who raised him, what else will?

After I told him, he said the one kind thing as he saw how upset I was. He made me call my best friend, Hallie.

He waited in silence as I cried and left when Hallie got there. She was the second person to learn the truth—that her very best friend had been lying through her privileged, straight teeth, paid for by good parents.

The only thing that I remember out of what I said during the time he was waiting in silence is, "Does that sound good to you? To just walk out of this door and never come back?"

CHAPTER 4

Sunday, January 7, 2024
(Three days later)

We're waiting for the DNA test results to prove he is not her father. It's like he's holding out hope that my story isn't true, and I don't think it gets any sadder than that. I told him that the test will confirm my story, unfortunately.

I'm realizing that I think the only rational plan is for Dawson to walk away, to get to build a new life and marry another woman. I know he can never be happy with me, especially now.

I must understand why I was willing to throw away everything (my moral values and my God-given potential) to try to gain Dawson's admiration to fulfill me. Knowing it was fire and ice, that he was a lion not meant to be tamed by me.

What do I know about how he feels though. Part of him is probably doing a happy dance since he never deemed me worthy of marriage. And part of him is *broken* over his love for Kya, and all he has now wasted to help her thrive thus far.

It is freeing to release him from the lies and my broken hopes and dreams in him. But it doesn't feel good that I have let him down even greater than he ever let me down now.

I have not seen Dawson since the clinic visit on Friday. He has shown potential for forgiveness and potential for a life in peace by his lack of immediate anger or shame or threats. It's almost like he's considering what I said, about staying in Kya and my life.

Dawson did ask for clarity on one specific: Did I get pregnant with the intent to play it off as his baby all along? Why did I choose a blonde German man with similar facial characteristics? He explained how this makes a big difference in what a jury would think of my fraud. While paternity fraud is not a punishable crime in the US, most women can claim they were surprised far after the birth. The story of planning to get pregnant and knowing the baby wasn't Dawson's before he signed the birth certificate takes it to a whole different realm of family-court filings.

I had a chance to explain to him that no one can ever break my story from the truth. Now that I can be completely honest. I can reassure everyone, that was not my plan at the beginning (to get pregnant with someone else and claim it as his child). My desired criteria for reproducing included "blonde," and this other man checked the box. He passed my test as being a kind and emotionally wise person on the date, and so I followed through with my plan to become a mom, alone. (Not a smart decision, but it's what I honestly remember thinking.)

And then I couldn't stop hanging out with Dawson while I had time left, even though I was newly pregnant. I really think I never would have told Dawson he was the father except that he noticed I was pregnant during sex, and it made it too easy to not want to break his heart in a different way, too easy to have one of my wildest dreams come true in a fake way.

When Dawson noticed my stomach and told *me* that I was pregnant and that my denial was a lie. I didn't say, "She's not yours," and so I don't know if that makes this *any* better at all.

I guess I felt like I had to stay living in the lie because of my own weaknesses and letting Satan control me. And I wanted him to be with me more than anything.

Dawson had just assumed the baby was his on that first day, and I never straight-out lied. I forgive myself for that. But on the second day at a fancy restaurant over mushroom ravioli, I became miserable the moment he said, "If it is my child, then the child will have my last name." I was now playing out a fiction novel and destroying my real life. The best ravioli ever, tasteless.

What I said about Dawson choosing if he wants to stay in Kya's life? That immediate considering of the option just shows his love for her. But I still imagine that the anger just hasn't set in yet for him and his family. That I will struggle in facing the world again, although I think it's possible now. Maybe the worst part is over? That was the first step in a bigger plan of saving my life (what's left of it, for my daughter).

Perhaps I was blind for asking him to please stay with me and Kya. There's no way he will choose it *now* if he wouldn't choose it with me back when I was a more honorable potential wife.

How can I wish for both? A new life with no lies means…a miracle? Forgiveness and deep reconciliation? Or is it freedom from the life that I thought I wanted with Dawson—and freedom from never being seen as an equal partner or worthy of respecting for marriage. I tell him that he is perfect even though I know he is not. He is to me. He's pretty close.

Whatever the case may be, I pray again today that this first step will catapult other goals of mine into motion, that I'll continue to feel this energy and strength as I tackle other obstacles holding me back.

Please help me, God. I have no idea what my future will hold. But I hope that I will just hold Kya and wait patiently, kindly, honestly, humbly, and in awe of the universe. My pain is so irrelevant to the greater plan here.

CHAPTER 5

Tuesday, January 9, 2024
(Five days later)

ANALISE: Before I tell the father, are you sure?
*Incoming call from Dawson.

ANALISE: I'm hopping in the shower, the neighbor said she can watch Kya. I'll be there as soon as I can.

Post-truth sinful sex no. 1.

I got to tell him that he was right the whole time, that he was better than me. That he was perfect to me. That his sister's eulogy notes during his dad's funeral—"Anyone who knows Dawson knows that his daddy taught him to serve the 'least of these'"—had a whole different meaning to me which I needed to be honest about.

I'm trying to tell myself that Dawson will never come back to me. That he will find a girl way more beautiful and younger. But I can try to love myself?

But what do I remember about seeing him?

We passionately kissed goodbye near his door.

I felt more comfortable in my naked skin than ever before.

I held him, and I learned that when Dawson cries, it isn't slow tears that fall out of his eyes or an ugly cry face. It's a deep groan as he gave up his fatherly love for Kya, like pain from his heart was shaking his whole body, and then it passed shortly after. Twice like that.

He said, "I missed you" (while we were making love? Or maybe lovesick), and it made me laugh at how absurd it was to hear him say.

He was pouring out grace to me and later referred to it as taking out frustration. But nothing seemed angry in that moment to me. Not sure if I'll ever see that GoPro footage myself or if he will ever watch it either. We both said "I love you" several times.

Getting to talk to him about this now is so unreal, it's like a dream.

He said, "You knew your whole life was a lie for two years. You have prepared for this moment, but I need help making sense of this."

I was happy to act strong for him tonight. I told him everything beautiful that I could think of, and I meant it. Maybe that's all he needed from me, and it's not that he ever considered coming back.

I said, "You will go to the Caribbean again next summer with your family, and maybe by then, you will smile again, and you will laugh again. Maybe you will own a dog one day, that is how much of a dad you will be again. Maybe you will watch more Netflix and take better care of yourself."

Meanwhile, I need to find out what Sven wants when he finds out that Kya exists.

CHAPTER 6

January 10, 2024
(Six days later)

DAWSON: Can you make this pain go away?

ANALISE: I wish, but I know after what I did, that you must start over now. You don't *want* to be her stepfather, right? I'm so angry at myself. Why did I throw away everything just for a fake chance to be involved with you and your perfect family, knowing you never valued me as a wife? What about the last name on her birth certificate? Your things still left at my house? Have you told your family or shared with the world at all? Do you plan to sue me? Do you want me to quit my job? Move away? Anything else? Why did you say you loved me during sex? Is there still a chance?

Dawson calls my parents to apologize for a weak moment in asking to see me. He mentions that his friend (a psychiatrist) deemed my texts as unstable, potentially hinting whether I am fit to be a mother.

I feel worse now. It's been six days since I told Dawson the truth. It's been only a few days since I told my parents also and asked them for space.

I started my new life. It doesn't feel like much of a life yet besides Kya's beauty. I was waiting on some word from Dawson on his next steps. My parents think he will retaliate...who knows?

Dawson is going to pick up his things. I lost every right to have a say in anything related to him. I can't call him. I can't text him. I can't embarrass him anymore. I can try to make him feel good if I'm blessed to be able to see him again, be it once or several times. I want to exemplify the Lord in the relationship starting *now*.

Notes from my biblical counselor:

Lean on people for support.

I am not a victim.

I listed to the Holy Spirit talking to me (finally).

The enemy will be mad that I told the truth and come after me, so be careful.

The center of my relationships should be Christ.

I am allowed to process, but not dwell.

Build my life, not on shame.

Why is it killing me waiting for what is going to happen next? I need to chill. This is my new life (ha-ha yay). Me and my Kya girl. Not waiting on anyone to bring us flowers.

This is a new start. God's mercies are new every morning.

Maybe not Dawson's mercy, but *your* mercy, God.

CHAPTER 7

Thursday, January 11, 2024
(One week later)

ANALISE: From your mom just now—"Hello, Analise, can I stop in San Francisco to see Kya tomorrow?" Do you want me to tell her for you, since you're dreading it?

DAWSON: I think you should plan to tell her—in person.

ANALISE: I will. Is your sister okay?

DAWSON: Both she and (her husband) both cried on the phone for a while.

ANALISE: For you. They love you so much, Dawson. It was a miserable life, if that helps at all.

CHAPTER 8

Friday, January 12, 2024
(Eight days later)

7:00 a.m.

> ANALISE: I'm so sorry I didn't realize that I could tell you sooner. And then throughout, knowing your dad was sick. I was sick every day from the position I put myself in, defeated. I tried not to hold you back from time with him, but I know it was all wrong. Part of me still thinks your dad getting sick could have been because of the evil I brought into your family. Like my punishment more than anything.
>
> DAWSON: Maybe God took my daddy home so that he didn't have to experience this much evil. Because he knows what it is like to be a father and would not be able to bear seeing a child ripped away from their "father."
>
> ANALISE: Yes, maybe. We will never know.

2:00 p.m.

> ANALISE: Your mom is here.
>
> DAWSON: I am available for her.

6:45 p.m.

> DAWSON: If you are going to come to me, let me know.
>
> ANALISE: (???) You're ill now. How can I get you help?
>
> DAWSON: Yeah, you spread it to me.

18

ANALISE: What's the one thing you tried to teach me. You are better than me. Set up some dates. I told your sister that you called me so that no one can say I am hurting you further. Please let me know you're okay.

He asked me to come over again, but I stupidly (and smartly) declined the invitation. I do regret...kind of. There aren't many big regrets besides what I did to Dawson. But I do regret calling his sister to tell her that I was worried that he is seeking intimacy from me during this time. Every part of me wants to go see him, but I don't understand.

Last time I saw him, when he asked to be intimate, I immediately starting crying. I said, "You must be ill." I knew he had the camera rolling. I thought maybe he was setting me up somehow. But he brought out the lingerie from back when I was young and innocent. He softly told me he needed this. He said, "I need help temporarily taking away the pain." If that is all that it is, I don't think I can help with that.

CHAPTER 9

Saturday, January 13, 2024
(Nine days later)

What a blur…

My parents showed up for a visit and took Kya with them, meaning I get to clean up my house and be lazy for two whole days.

I got to talk to his mom for an hour in person yesterday, to explain what happened. She understood my foolishness somehow. The rumor is that she immediately tried to tell Dawson to forgive me, creating quite a divide between his mother and siblings. I do not find pleasure in that angle, although I appreciate her unconditional support in my life after what I did to her family.

I need to get my freaking crap together. He's moving on. Forever. As he deserves.

He was not happy with me, and I lied to him for two years. He put everything he had into being a good dad, and I watched that.

It's too late for me to be with the man of my dreams (Dawson) in a healthy relationship.

To do: Wake up, forgive myself, exercise, do good things for people and move on. And stop making the same mistakes. (Note: I did not take my own advice here yet.)

10:00 p.m.

ANALISE: Are you okay?
DAWSON: What do you think?

Post-truth sinful sex no. 2.

CHAPTER 10

ANALISE: I will trust that you know where you can reach me, and with that, wish you nothing but the best from here. I have about $35,000 in savings that I'm comfortable sending your way right now. I've reimbursed all but $5,000 of the other funds you ever shared. But like I said, I know you know how to reach me.

DAWSON: You can make it feel better.

ANALISE: After what I did to you, it made me deadly ill, and I feel less ill now that I'm honest with you. I can't take advantage anymore. I just want to make sure you were okay.

DAWSON: You can take away this hurt.

Post-truth sinful sex no. 3.

This time together we went across the street to grab drinks and food at the bar. He told me that I looked wonderful when I arrived.

Dawson did some shaming to make me feel like a whore, but it is true. In some of the ways I acted, I have surely earned myself the title. I tried to explain to him that it's not an excuse for my lies, but… When I acted as a whore in that moment, trying to get pregnant with Sven, was that a greater sin to God than the approximately two hundred times Dawson had pulled out of me during sex because he didn't want to commit to marriage and children? *Wasn't this the only argument (not to excuse sin) for a couple wanting to recover from infidelity?* To both accept that needs were not being met. But if you work to rekindle the willingness to meet needs and commit fully to one another once again, it could still result in a relationship of one's dreams. *That could only happen if mutual sin was recognized and sins were not weighted.* That was the point of the analogy. Not that anything could ever rationalize what I did.

He says, "Why did God have to choose me to help you become a better person?"

I feel like I explained my perspective on how this evil spiraled out of control because of shared sin at first. But I realize that sounds like I am trying to rationalize my lie, and I don't want to do that either. It's just my honest answer to his question, not that he deserved to waste two years of his life in this situation.

There's nothing weirder than our magical, beautiful sex now though. It feels so good to be able to say sorry and submit to him completely. I mean it, completely. *But it's still sin. What are you trying to teach me now, God? The same thing as before, again?*

CHAPTER 11

Flashback No. 1

2020–2022
(The two years prior to telling the lie)

Let's go back and think like the Analise who existed a few years earlier. When I was in my late prime midtwenties.

Queue the early dating memories: football games, Christmas-tree farms, boating on the coast, kissing and being silly in the mirror, etc.

An intimate passion that, ideally, would have been felt only among a healthy engaged couple or newlyweds in a sacred union. Also, including the following:

- God's strength in both individuals
- Understanding of their unique value to one another
- Mature expectations
- Baseline conflict-resolution skills that are later needed in said romantic relationships

That was not the case here.

I fell in love with Dawson in 2020, four years ago now. Two years were fair dating; two, I lied.

If I close my eyes and I try to describe to you what it was like to meet him, the reference to character Christian Grey helps. Dawson was a bit older than me; had more money than me; and was raised by smarter, healthier parents in certain ways.

Early on into dating him, we were at a small get-together at my friend's apartment overlooking the skyline. Dawson and his friend came to the party talking about Z-scores, or a girl's number on a value scale. It combined looks, family, personality, career, fitness, etc.

My friend whispered, "Man, these guys really think they are better than everyone else, huh?"

Sadly, the red flags drew me in. I thought, *I am valuable, and I like a good challenge. I benefit him too, right?*

The dates and time we spent together during the first few weeks in San Francisco felt like a fairy tale. He was a real-life angel for me after my high-school sweetheart and I parted ways.

I thought Dawson thought our connection was drop-dead special too. I knew I was far younger than other girls he had dated, so I assumed that I was way more fun. My job was badass. I would be climbing the corporate ladder in no time. What else did he and I need besides the blessing of a biblical marriage and a baby? I was sure we were on the same page.

We went to his friend Winn's beach house on the coast of Malibu after three full weeks of dating. This is where I got the nickname Analise—(Anal)ise.

Yes, I gladly gave him every part of me. In the bathroom mirror and looking over the water. Later that night, he named my alter party ego "Anal-ise." Everyone laughed at the great joke, which only I understood as an earned title, more than an imaginary one.

For the young girls and women listening: it is only a husband, who loves his wife and gives himself up for her, who should ever earn that position. It was me who I destroyed in that moment—setting myself up for a bond and obsession that was one-sided, signing my name to love him up until death, or risking acting insane because he didn't feel it too.

The great sex continued our whole relationship—well, no, not in that other hole. At least not again until after I told him the truth. (Excuse me for skipping ahead in the story, we'll get there soon. Learning the lesson the hard way again). Point being that the *normal* kind of sex still caused me the same, desperate, clingy, hopeless, sick love for him. He was the first man to ever make me orgasm, but our contract was not that I would be the first and or last woman to please him.

After six months of living my own real-life fairy tale with Dawson, even though he wasn't perfect, I wanted to be his girlfriend. It was Valentine's Day. He got dinner, and I brought the red lingerie and confidence to try a lap dance for the first time to some music. I thought

I did great. But he turned down my offer to put a title on it, and I stormed out.

The next week he was hooking up with the hottest bikini model in our city. She was a part of his elite friend group.

I didn't find out until a few weeks later when their fling had ended or was ending.

I had been getting my nails done and bumped into one of Dawson's friend's girlfriends. That is how I learned about his relationship with her. Apparently, the story goes, they both agreed it was just for fun. She had two older sons, and Dawson wasn't interested in taking that on.

As I was sitting in the nail salon, we were texting and hanging out again by that time. So back to one of his recent texts, I just said *her name*, question mark.

He called me a few times. I ignored and went to the grocery store, crying for some ice cream. I had been texting a few other people too, including a cute fighter pilot and a veterinarian. But the difference was, I was the one who asked to be his girlfriend and he said no. How could he not see my value?

When I finally did pick up his call, his explanation was that he was sorry, he just didn't feel the fireworks he was looking for based on our time together. The *exact* opposite of what I took away from our intimacy.

Hint: This is where shit in my life really hit the fan. I started to act truly irrationally with Dawson at this point. I should have let him go and realigned with Jesus at *this point*.

But instead, I coped from the news of him being with another girl, after denying becoming officially boyfriend/girlfriend with me, by getting a small boob job. Maybe now I could offer what must have been missing in his eyes. Well, she had both a boob job and a recent vagina job. I didn't even know that was a thing until I also learned about it in the nail salon. She walked funny for a few days afterward, but it was paid for by some rich old man in Houston that she saw occasionally. Apparently, the procedure included some snipping as well as sucking fat out of her back to put into the walls of her...well, you know.

The model later messaged me on Instagram to inform me that Dawson had showed her a video of me on his cell phone. He was standing up in the video, and I was in red lingerie on my knees. She wanted me to know that he didn't deserve to have that video of me. Heartbroken at the betrayal, I still stupidly wanted him to be the one to fix it.

Dawson would always call me back, with that deep, sexy confident voice of his, and take me to drinks to catch up. Sometimes in my part of town, sometimes his. Sometimes cold drinks on his roof overlooking the city and sometimes warm hot toddies and walking back to my six-hundred-square-foot apartment.

It was around two years that we had this type of on-and-off relationship. I cooked food for us and cleaned his place some. We went to church together, and I mostly did add fun to activities. Some pouting and demanding for sure thrown in by me. I tried my best to get through to him about opening his mindset around marriage. He seemed committed in every other way, so I struggled with that. I stormed out of his house at least once a week, because the intimacy didn't also include the meeting of my security/commitment needs with him.

It seemed frustrating to me that during reconciliation, we always had to focus on how irrational my behavior was (storming out or getting angry). We could never address that maybe I had a valid concern in his unwillingness to put a ring on my finger.

If I had been a stronger young woman when I met him and he wasn't trying to teach me both self-worth and healthy conflict resolution at the same time as playing the boyfriend role, maybe I would have been good enough for him. But probably not. I don't know why he kept coming around, honestly.

The most insane part is this flashback doesn't represent Dawson at all anymore. The man who brought me so much pain has now turned into the dream man. He's so logical and willing to compromise (on most things). The next girl to have him is a lucky one. I was a lucky one too while I had him. He taught me everything that I do know about love now, even if he would never commit to me.

As I look back on any situation where I feel like Dawson wronged me previously, it's just to try and explain how and why I think that I *drove myself* insane. Maybe other people will interpret this as wrong of me to share in the story. But again, I am trying to help you understand why I made the terrible decision to lie. The lying was built on several other bad decisions including sex outside of marriage and not trusting God fully with my life.

Dawson is a strong man who will carry on his father's legacy well (like how he's handling this situation with any grace at all).

Point of clarity being is that Dawson is not the villain in this book. I hate that he is a part of this story now at all.

CHAPTER 12

An Anthem During Flashback No. 1

2021

As a generational stereotype, I've grown up with Swift albums spanning decades, as every decade my own personal heartbreaks became worse. Now, Taylor should write a song about the hurt that Dawson is allowed to feel at this point. I took a big mess and made an even bigger one.

I strongly encourage you to pause and listen to the entire song. I felt as though it was the story of my life when the new version came out in 2021:

♫ "All Too Well" (ten-minute version) by Taylor Swift

Back before I betrayed my honor, I could honestly say I thought I was standing up for God in our relationship. I was able to say, "How is it, that I can love you and tell you that you are my one... even though you are imperfect. But it isn't the same way around. You see my imperfections and do not love all of me regardless. This is not love. How, how, is this just sex to you? I think I am good enough for you. I think I am beautiful enough for you. You are all I want. You have the potential to be the father and husband that I've dreamed of. But you don't pick me to be your wife."

But fast-forward one year when I lied to him. I was so weak and sick, ignoring my potential and blessed path forward.

There are no excuses for what I did to Dawson in the aftermath of this hurt. But if I could go back in time as a younger girl, I would realize that the destruction that comes from sex outside of marriage is not worth the thrill. The reward that comes from doing this the way God intended is far greater of a goal and method to follow than a worldly, Hollywood view.

I cannot rationalize the lie that I told to Dawson. But I can admit that I could have stopped the negative spiral sooner if I realized that I didn't *need* Dawson to recognize my value *if I believed it myself.*

Even though I picked up on something in Dawson's family that I wanted, which was different from the life my parents led, I could have used it to build a life of my own, as an honorable and suitable potential wife. And left it alone after a fair dating effort on my part.

But I didn't know how to move on past Dawson not wanting to marry me after our sex. I wanted *him* to confirm my value, and I went temporarily insane for it. I let Satan control my life.

I have reflected now on other small lies I had told previously in my life and how those small ones also never turned out good. I wish it didn't take such a huge one to teach me my lesson once and for all on God's moral laws. They're set before us to encourage our own thriving.

Growing up, I attended fourteen different schools across four states in K–12th grade. That can do different things to different kids, but for me, it trained me to walk into a room of people and be anyone that I wanted confidently as hell. This was only temporary after all, may as well live it to the fullest? I should have not let my strength be what destroyed me, but I did.

This is not quite the life I meant to create for myself and my child from my overwhelmingly blessed upbringing. I'm on my way to a better place now, at least. But I'm still relearning how to trust God fully and sanctify myself. The definition of *sanctify* is to become more holy.

CHAPTER 13

Flashback No. 2

2011–2018
(Ages before I made the decision to lie)

As a young teenage girl, I thought I was going to change the world for the better in a big way. Never did I dream that the Award for the Best Lie would go to me.

No. I messed up my life. I got caught up somewhere I didn't belong, and I betrayed the God I knew *but did not fully fear.*

I wrote down so many beautiful quotes and excerpts to myself as a young girl, from 2015 to 2021. Here are examples:

> Sagittarius: Strong pillars to lean on. Supportive of others, good teachers. Caring but not overly involved. Independent, capable of anything they put their minds to.

> For what shall it profit a man, if he shall gain the whole world, and lose his own soul? (Mark 8:36)

This one was my favorite, even though it's exactly what I ended up doing.

> You're as pretty as you treat people.

I find this one funny now because it was another one of my favorites when I always felt like the hottest girl in the room. Now I feel as though God took away my beauty for living in sin.

As you get older, you realize that you're not always right and there were so many situations you could have handled better, so many times you could have been kinder. But all you can really do is forgive yourself and let your mistakes make you a better person.

Unless it's mad, passionate, extraordinary love, it's a waste of time. There are many mediocre things in life and love is not one of them. You're too full of life to be half-loved.

One day you'll wake up at 11:30 a.m. on a Saturday with the love of your life and you will make some coffee and pancakes and it will be alright.

I want to grow up and be generous and bighearted, the way that people have been with me.

Love is about appreciation; love is not about possession.

She was beautiful, for the way she thought. She was beautiful, for the sparkle in her eyes when she talked about something she loved. She was beautiful, for her ability to make other people smile, even if she was sad. No, she wasn't beautiful for something as temporary as her looks. She was beautiful, deep down to her soul.

Most importantly, love. Like it's the only thing you know how. At the end of the day, everything means nothing, your degree, your job, the money... Nothing matters except for love and human connection —who you loved and how deeply you loved them. How much you touched the people around you and how much you gave to them.

How we experience change is up to us. It can feel like a death grip or a second chance at life. If we open our fingers, loosen our grip, it can feel like pure adrenaline. Like at any moment we can have another chance at life. (*Grey's Anatomy*)

When you feel like things should be different, remember the valleys and mountains which have gotten you here. Those moments are not in vain or accidents. You are not the same. You are grown and you are growing. You are wrapped in endless, boundless grace and things *will* get better. For there is more to you than yesterday. (Morgan Harper Nichols)

One day, God will meet you in heaven. You don't want him to greet you with a vision and say, "Here is what you could have done. This is who you could have been." Truly becoming the person that He called you to be is not easy, but it will be so worth it. You want Him to greet you with, "Well done, my good and faithful servant." So, promise yourself—to take the chance to change before it's too late.

My god, I hope you find love. And I don't just mean that in regard to someone you wrap your tired bones around at night. I mean that I hope you find love in every aspect of your life. I hope you find it tucked into early morning sunrises, and the smell of your favorite places. I hope you find it strung between the laughter you share with your friends, I hope it bounces off you when you hug the people you care for, I hope it swells within your ribcage whenever you hear your favorite song or discover something that moves you. I hope you fall in love with growth, and change, and the messiness and the beauty of screwing up, and making mistakes, and becoming exactly who you want to be. I hope you find love in places that were once void of it, in places within yourself that you could have been softer to, kinder to, in the past. Because if there is one thing I have learned, it is that love is so much more than a boy, or a girl, who holds your heart. Love is everything around you. It is everything. (Bianca Sparacino, *A Gentle Reminder*)

Occasionally, weep deeply over the life that you hoped would be. Grieve the losses. Then wash your face. Trust God. And embrace the life you have. (John Piper)

I like living. I have sometimes been wildly, despairingly, acutely miserable, racked with sorrow; but through it all, I still knew quite certainly that just to be alive is a grand thing. (Agatha Christie)

You can't create chaos in the lives of others and expect peace to come to yours. No matter what they did or how you feel, causing others to hurt will never bring healing to you. (Morgan Richard)

When was the last time that you were truly grateful to be alive? Being fully awake to the passing of the day and night, fully feeling your existence. Gratitude isn't something you think into being. It's something you feel—being alive. Recognizing your heart beating for you on this beautiful planet. Gratitude comes from what is, not what might be.

But one of the most ironic, I wrote down on May 6, 2021. Right before the boob job, around nine months before I lied to Dawson, falling into an even deeper pit of misery. I hope he finds comfort in these words now:

When someone betrays you, it's a reflection of their character, not yours. Only hurt people hurt other people. True forgiveness is when you can say thank you for that experience even though you didn't deserve to know me in the way that you did. (Iyjerria)

CHAPTER 14

An Anthem During Flashback No. 2

2011

I encourage you to pause and listen to this old song:

♫ "Take a Bow" by Rihanna

I heard this old banger on the radio the other day. If you were reading Dawson's journal instead of mine, I imagine it would sound something like that song.

He taught her to walk. He taught her to say "Dada." Think of the thousands of photos he took during that time and how Apple will not let him forget those memories unless he deletes them. He deserves the sympathy, not me.

I've been trying to honestly ask myself, considering *all* angles of this math from a more enlightened state:

1. Initially, I felt so wronged by Dawson so early on, yet I tragically loved him and was obsessed in our future together.
2. I made the decision to get pregnant and be a mother alone, or so was the original plan. Completely *in spite of* his reluctance to give me what I asked for in the relationship (a life commitment, not just passionate sex and dating).
3. I made the terrible decision to lie to Dawson.

Was it payback? Am I that evil? I can tell you, I didn't intend it to be.

Somehow, I just selfishly picked "more time with Dawson" in my head at that moment when he noticed the bump and made it easier for the truth of my baby to be known to him.

The whole time I was living the lie, I thought, *When I am dead, everyone will cling to the twisted, psycho love factor idea. Like I was just so in love with Dawson that I set up my life and trapped him in it.*

I can tell you what I do remember feeling every day. I felt pure internal panic from the moment after lying. Cuss words to myself were said every morning I remembered for the first time, and every night, trying to fall asleep, thinking, *What have I done? I want to die. But I love my baby.* And right then, at four months pregnant, it did feel a tiny bit good to have him hold me for a while at least, even though I was also miserable about it. I know it doesn't make sense.

I loved him, and now he looked at me kind of differently, *more respected. This would surely all end after he takes the planned DNA test after birth*, I thought. But in fact, my sin was a weight on my shoulder much longer than those few months. The longer I stayed in the lie, the harder it was to get out and the worse it felt.

Of course, I can't deny that the selfish reasons I lied to Dawson included all the status of who he is, not just my hopeless love for him. There were benefits to more time with Dawson and the world thinking that he was my baby daddy. I guess that's why it took so long to tell the truth.

CHAPTER 15

Thursday, January 18, 2024
(Two weeks later)

I am extremely sad and overwhelmed. Maybe *depressed* is the word. But also, I am less depressed than when I was lying somehow. Each day is supposed to be a new chance for me to find peace with God, but I haven't fully arrived there. I know that I *will*.

Kya has been sick, teething, missing Dawson, and not loving the cold weather. She is using up all my energy, and that is okay. I am so sorry I made these decisions and for every lie I told that destroyed me. The consequences don't only affect me.

Why am I still sad that he is gone? He deserves that.

4:00 p.m.

DAWSON: When is a good time to chat?

DAWSON: Okay, I'll reach out then. Not urgent. Really sad.

ANALISE: But you should be relieved. You can rest, relax, put yourself first for once. Or you know you want to be a daddy now, so you get to go do it on your own terms with the perfect lady to spoil you and fulfill you. Or Kya and I are still alive and still here, she or I can try to make you happy?

DAWSON: Losing love for a daughter is not walking away. And you have no idea how much this has hurt me.

ANALISE: I'm sorry. It hurts me to have hurt you too. I will look forward to talking to you. You're going to be just fine, sweet man.

CHAPTER 16

Friday, January 19, 2024
(Two weeks, one day later)

> Dawson sends *routing number* for bank account.
> *Goodbye to my life savings.*
> *Fully rational to buy himself a new truck after what he just went through in my opinion.*

DAWSON: Did you talk to him?

ANALISE: I did. I just met with him in person. Very difficult, but also, all of this is better than the life I had while I was lying to you. I know this will hurt to read for you. I am very, very sad right now as well.

DAWSON: When can you tell me what he said? Clean yourself up. I'm at the gym. Trying not to cry.

ANALISE: I am not going to be able to come see you tonight. I feel ill.

*Incoming call from Dawson.

ANALISE: Here at door downstairs.

Post-truth sinful sex no. 4.

This is the last time he recorded the entire interaction of us together on his GoPro. Hearing him say I am the sexiest woman to him hurts and feels good. I just wish he wanted me to be his wife. He must want that now because of this response, right? We listened to the song that was playing in his car the moment I met him, and I said, "Oh my gosh, this is my favorite song right now!"

The rest of the weekend, our texts read...

Saturday, January 20, 2024

DAWSON: I need you to make sure that he will take a DNA test.

ANALISE: He said he would.

Sunday, January 21, 2024

DAWSON: I am wholly broken over this day that Kya will be "trying" for a daddy... You can't imagine how awful this is for her and (less important but) for me. My soul is broken, and spirit is crushed by you.

ANALISE: Today's sermon, Pastor Chad talked about Jezebel, the prostitute who brings illness on those she was impure with. And fatherlessness or that type of sin leading to rhetorical downfall of nations. It was relevant to say the least. The past two days have been the worst. Kya has missed you. It is pain so deep. The man she is meeting today is not you, and your presence in her life will impact her for the better *forever* (I hope). And I hope the same for you. I'm trying to be strong for Kya, and you, and myself today. I don't know what this man wants or will be to her. But when I met with him, he said he does not care what her last name is, and so Kya is mine. I hope this is another person to bring good to her eventually. Sending you my "I'm sorry" this morning.

DAWSON: You are not only my Jezebel, but you are also the serpent to my Garden of Eden.

ANALISE: Not joking. One time over summer when I was at Hallie's, there was a huge snake lingering on her front steps that was suffocating a rat, and I knew it was a sign from God to me. It's so weird to reflect now. Stupid decision and severely impaired thinking. A split second of strength to tell the truth in what I sometimes felt was just a cursed life. Telling the truth has brought on such enlightened realizations about my lack of healthy adult relating and poor motivations in dating. All my childhood experience, my personality and ambition all hitting this spiral when I was knowing you. The evil unraveled. I'm honored to be alive and feel a completely new for the most part. Like my chains broke. I'm sad, but I'm not ill right now. I was ill for two years, if not before then. But it isn't about me. You got this today hang in there. I hope that you realize every possibility in life is yours again! I know everybody will encourage you to simply find a worthy woman and move on for your best interest. But why are you tormenting yourself so much in this in-between? Wanting to be her Dada and so sad. You are her legal father, and you're the only one who's going to change that now, which again, makes sense...But from what I am hearing, if you said, "I *want* to be her father," everyone would respect that too. Kya would just maybe have another dad who's not as cool as you. *But Dawson!* We can file those papers, go before the court, and get you out as soon as possible. That makes sense. You're not picking to say, "I want to restart life with you and Kya even though there is a real father in the picture." Sven asked me if that was the case, and I said 99 percent of me thinks you want to walk away. But 1 percent of you is struggling. Just be brave to pick, be sure, and move on. Thank you for being so good to me, but I can't help you heal by ever sinning again. You know that. I love you. And I am not the beautiful woman that I once was either. The illness took a toll on my body, health, aged me, and made me hideous from inside out. You just remember that. A lot of girls are hotter than me now.

DAWSON: You made the decision. You chose to loot my heart by extorting my goodness with a child. I allowed your evil to enter my heart and be destructive to the deepest part of what it is to be a man.

ANALISE: We will talk later. Go be magnificent, sweet man.

DAWSON: Make sure you tell him about all these nights.

Sends videos of he and Kya—jumping on the bed with her hair blowing in the fan, eating watermelon up at the lake house, her first nap on his chest, his first time holding her, her first time standing up.

Kya saw the pictures over my shoulder and screamed, "Dada!" So excited to see him. It was my own punishment to see her fall to the floor in distress as I turned off the screen. She wondered where he went and why he left her, her no. 1 person besides me. That's the only night she's ever slept thirteen hours for me.

DAWSON: Did you tell Kya that the person there tonight was her dada?

ANALISE: No, we did not say the word *dada*. When he was saying goodbye, I asked what to call him, and he said Sven. I asked Sven to apologize to his mother for me in this. He said, "I enjoyed meeting Kya. I would like to get more comfortable with her. I need to seek for a new job and see what my schedule will be like. Maybe we could pick a day in the week to start." But he also has made it clear, he thinks it's best for her to be with her mom. So he's not going away. But he doesn't have much money, so I don't see him getting lawyers involved. He just wants a chance to get to know her. She's so cute, you can't blame him. He openly said he respects whatever decision that you make, and he knows that it could change things for him. Anyways, I know you're likely not considering that. You would have to want to forgive me, marry me, and be a stepfather who must share his daughter. However, your texts the other night confused me. Go relax and watch gun videos. You are a good man, and you are doing great, but you are wasting too many days. You need to pick.

CHAPTER 17

Wednesday, January 24, 2024
(Three weeks later)

DAWSON: I'm not better. We should chat sometime soon.

ANALISE: No, you are wrong. You will see the good one day. Why are you angry at God and not leaning on him for peace? As for me, I screwed up. All I could do was start over and try to be a good mom. You need to do what's best for you as far as contacting me anymore or not.

DAWSON: See, the difference is you don't lose Kya…you will never understand. And you were not the one betrayed. My world is ending.

ANALISE: Move on to what is better. Not a minute more of yours wasted. Your eternal soul is calling, baby, just answer. Say yes.

DAWSON: Are you free today? Either you can come meet with me, or I can come see Kya. My lawyers have advised me not to see Kya, but that doesn't mean that I can't.

ANALISE: I'm completely shocked. I didn't know lawyers mattered in your decision to see her. I can let the neighbor watch her so we can talk.

Post-truth sinful sex no. …losing count.

CHAPTER 18

Saturday, January 27, 2024
(3.5 weeks later)

It's been twenty-three days.

A lot of good things are happening.

I started eating again. I might be eating too much. Cutting down on budget means more bread and pasta.

I went back to the office over the last few weeks. I knew layoffs were pending. One-half of my team was cut last week, but I survived. I know I am good at my job, so I knew I shouldn't be too scared. But also, God is too gracious for letting me keep the job amidst everything going on in my life. Now I need to crank out some work.

Kya has gotten more comfortable around her real father, Sven. She is starting to like him. He's been nothing but gentle and kind, interested in her flourishing. The world is made (more) right by this.

I know the years while Kya is young will strain me physically and mentally, but I am trying to enjoy her. All morning I got to be silly with her and make her laugh.

My happy ending is eternal life with Jesus. I *still* have a lot of work to do to repent, turn away from all sin, and cleanse my heart.

CHAPTER 19

Valentine's Day Week
(Five weeks later)

Thursday, February 8, 2024

Dawson sends iPhone video curated of all photos of us together and lyrics of the song "All Along, I Had It All." I can see how he thinks that song applies, even though I would disagree.

I sent a photo of Hallie, engaged as of today on her ski trip, with comment: "Your turn!"

Dawson sends an image of a Bible verse describing a wife:

> An excellent wife, who can find? She is far more precious than jewels. The heart of her husband trusts in her, and he will have no lack of gain. She does him good, and not harm, all the days of her life. She seeks wool and flax and works with willing hands. She is like the ships of the merchant; she brings her food from afar. She rises while it is yet night and provides food for her household and portions for her maidens. She considers a field and buys it; with the fruit of her hands, she plants a vineyard. She dresses herself with strength and makes her arms strong. She perceives that her merchandise is profitable. Her lamp does not go out at night. She puts her hands to the distaff, and her hands hold the spindle. She opens her hand to the poor and reaches out her hands to the needy. She is not afraid of snow for her household, for all her household are clothed in scarlet. She makes bed coverings for herself; her clothing is fine linen and purple. Her husband is known in the gates when he sits among the elders of the land. She makes

linen garments and sells them; she delivers sashes to the merchant. Strength and dignity are her clothing, and she laughs at the time to come. She opens her mouth with wisdom, and the teaching of kindness is on her tongue. She looks well to the ways of her household and does not eat the bread of idleness. Her children rise and call her blessed; her husband also, and he praises her: "Many women have done excellently, but you surpass them all." Charm is deceitful, and beauty is vain, but a woman who fears the LORD is to be praised. Give her of the fruit of her hands, and let her works praise her in the gates. (Proverbs 31:10–31)

Sunday, February 11, 2024
(During the Super Bowl)

DAWSON: Does that make you want to roller-skate?

ANALISE: I'm not watching. The head of the UCLA Marketing Department is on CNN to talk about the commercials (the lady I worked for during college). She's been trying to get me to come back and get involved on a junior advisory board.

DAWSON: Wow, that's crazy!

ANALISE: I don't care about the football game. I have been binge watching *The Crown*. Princess Diana is all I care about right now.

DAWSON: Diana was a nutcase. She was schizophrenic.

ANALISE: Who's your favorite celebrity, huh? Taylor Swift?

DAWSON: Travis and she are nothing more than a publicity stunt.

ANALISE: You could go to Netflix with your life story and get an hour-long documentary. Then every rich, hot woman in America might pity you. I have laughed out loud a few times since telling you the truth…To think about how I remember thinking, *I am exactly the type of person that people want to watch a one-hour documentary on.* Just to cringe at the screwed up the lens I saw the world through. At least I didn't murder anyone, but what I did isn't much better. I really believed there was going to be a documentary about my terrible being of a person. But I thought I would be dead too.

DAWSON: I have had requests from people to tell my story, but I did not think it would be good to ruin your life.

ANALISE: Sometimes I think being found guilty of fraud, losing my job, and having to be a burden on my parents would be easier than trying to go on as normal in some ways. So if that's what you want, I can quit. I also think, what if I had died with this secret? What if somehow you never found out. You just had a daughter that is a little bit shorter than she should be. Or if I had run away and you spent more years with Kya alone until you found out. Just so insane to think how it could have been even worse.

DAWSON: No, I don't want you to quit your job. That is what is best for Kya. Stop asking about that. And yes, mental disorders are complicated.

ANALISE: I said, Bye Felicia (or bye, Satan).

DAWSON: Are you showered now? I'm only seven minutes away from your place.

February 14, 2024
(Valentine's Day)

Well, I had a month and ten days of thinking the result of this would be a miracle: Dawson somehow wanting to stay with me and be Kya's dada by choice. I've not properly grieved and felt my feelings of loss and regret because I had hope. We have seen each other seven or eight times since the day I told him the truth. Each time only getting more passionate. But this week is Valentine's, a reality check. Who is he getting dinner with tonight? Probably not me. It's 6:30 p.m., and I'm still at the office.

Dawson didn't text back yesterday after I said, "You would know by now if your decision was one other than the obvious one, walking away." I told him we can't keep sinning together. I texted his sister trying to gauge her thoughts on seeing him. Her lack of response tells me that this was supposed to be a secret. Dawson was relying on me for support, but he was never considering coming back.

I'm not excited about the blank slate yet. Sure, I never have to beg him to respect me, love me, commit to me ever again. And I should stop giving all of myself to him if I am trying to trust God now.

I hope Dawson is getting dinner tonight with some pretty lady. I even gave our cute young doctor his number earlier this week when I confessed the truth to her. I told her she should check on him and take her shot in landing a perfect Christian husband. Maybe it would work out better for her.

I get to go home and see Kya at least.

February 15, 2024

DAWSON: I was sad because I did not hear from you yesterday. Your flowers are at my house. White roses are your favorite, right?

CHAPTER 20

Sunday, February 18, 2024
(Six weeks later)

Dawson asked to see Kya today.

When we arrived at the park, Dawson was already on a swing facing the other direction. As we walked closer and Kya could see who it was, she yelled "Dada" at the top of her lungs. Then as he got up and walked toward her slowly, she froze and acted shy. She knew something was different about him. He came up to hug her. I tried to hold back my tears to see their deep hug. It had been over forty days. I wish I took a video now, perhaps the last time they'd ever see each other.

We went out to eat dinner, and it was fun. I can't afford restaurant food anymore, so I appreciated the chance to eat fancy salmon and vegetables.

As we were waiting for our table, the bartender said, "Oh my goodness, y'all did great, she is so cute. Picasso."

We laughed.

CHAPTER 21

Flashback No. 3

August 2023
(Five months prior to telling the truth)

I made it to Florida, but then I chickened out. I didn't get on my connecting flight to the Caribbean (to meet Dawson and his family). I belong at home with Kya. I spent another small fortune to catch the next flight back to San Francisco.

Dawson wasn't surprised. I had told him goodbye and didn't take him up on the offer to join originally. But I figured last minute that the Caribbean would be a good place to find somewhere to drown myself.

I guess I will have to come up with something else. Better not ruin their vacation.

CHAPTER 22

Monday, February 26, 2024
(Almost two months later)

ANALISE: Do you want to see her again to say goodbye?

DAWSON: Analise, I do want to see her. You made it so that me seeing her is contingent on your wants. Stop trying to manipulate me. Goodbye.

ANALISE: Me: Is there any chance you love me too, and want to come home to Kya?

You: Stop manipulating me.

I don't know what demon possessed you (from the beginning of this relationship) to interpret me genuinely asking your interest in marriage is manipulation. My bad. Since you're so into the idea of a woman not having to ask you about marriage, maybe next time you ask her first. You are right. I was never supposed to ask. Just to leave you based on your disinterest a long time ago.

UPDATE: (on *hold* for unique candidate, forty-five days).

Position closed: Full-time father and lover centered on God in south part of town.

Reason closed: No verbal interest received from candidate.

Further action required: find new F-buddy.

DAWSON: Speaking of "Further action," I saw your *F-buddy* last night. I think he was busing tables or something. What a great father *you* picked.

ANALISE: He seems very kind, so that's good for Kya. But how unfortunate, how small of a world. He told me yesterday was his first day at a new job. Hope you enjoyed church today as much as I did.

Analise 2.0 would have loved if you had a different decision yesterday. But I can't say I'm surprised.

DAWSON: Don't quit your job. No decision was made. You should have thought about that before fucking a stranger. But you did not think. You fucked. Up. And by that, I mean down.

1.0 fucks stranger.

2.0 gets mad at Dawson because she fucked a stranger.

Can't wait for 3.0.

ANALISE: I'm so glad that I made a huge life mistake and learned from it. So I will never have to be your age and still be stupid as hell and not be happily married. We're so much better off without you, since you are not sure. This situation has not brought you to your knees with God from my perspective. So funny that what I felt for the past fifty days was one sided. It reminded me how I got so fucked up from you.

DAWSON: I'm not the reason you're fucked up. Good night.

ANALISE: When I'm married one day, I will forever remember what you taught me. Thank you.

Later this night, he called me. We got dinner and went back to my place since Kya is gone with my parents.

Post-truth sinful sex no. 10—the final lesson.

I stopped midway through crying, and he left. I kept telling him to find a wife and that I thought he was going to regret losing me one day.

I need to finally do the right thing with my body. Walking with God means eliminating sex outside of marriage—for real this time.

My breasts have been aching because he made my breast milk come back in.

"It's good for me," he says.

Again, I would agree if he were my husband.

CHAPTER 23

Tuesday, February 27, 2024
(Almost two months later)

3:00 p.m.

*Text to *Dawson's mother and sister*, as I sat in a hotel room, traveling for work in Colorado.

ANALISE: Hello. Let me start out with I'm sorry, and heartbroken for what I did to Dawson, although I repented for my sin. I'm reaching out to ask for help (yes, if you can believe it, I have the audacity). I have waited around fifty days holding his open position as a father to Kya. His uncertainty and responses as I share my enlightened views and newfound self-respect says everything. I have begged to be able to marry him and build a new life with him, giving him all I can in love and sacrifice from here on out. But throughout the fifty days, his lack of moving forward or coming to any bold moves makes me realize that his heart needs to be freed for something else. And I will also be freed to pursue marriage elsewhere. As much as I wish Dawson wanted it with me too after all this. My request for help is to see that he's okay as I set up my parameters and am forced to cut off friendship or dating with him or whatever this is called. We have had sex over ten times in the last fifty days. Please oversee he is okay. I will wait until the end of the day for his last confirmation. That his role should not be held open any longer. With your help, I hope we can convince him he's allowed to say yes (*if he wants*), or no if he wants. I'm waiting. But he can't expect me to allow him to not be sure forever in this position with Kya and me. Dawson sees my heart's offer as manipulation, and I hope you will understand I'm going to let another woman fight that battle now. Part of what drove me mad was trying to convince Dawson that I was valuable. But I'm done even though I hate the outcome. I guess I am showing imperfection and weakness in the aftermath of this. Thanks and sorry.

6:40 p.m.

DAWSON: I am not healed from what you did to me.
ANALISE: So do you want me to be the one to heal it or not? Are you going to answer or not?

11:00 p.m.

DAWSON: You have said your piece before. We are not going to have a future. You made these decisions for us. Do not contact me or my family anymore, or there will be paperwork delivered to you. (Blocks Analise.)

Analise calls suicide hotline number, screaming and crying loud enough for neighboring hotel rooms to hear her. (A new low).

ANALISE (to his sister's phone): Will you tell him that I want to kill myself if he's really going to do this and block me. I have been on the phone with the suicide hotline, and I would really ask if you could have him call me right now.

CHAPTER 24

Flashback No. 4

October 2023
(Three months prior to telling the truth)

*A goodbye-ish letter for Kya, in case I finally did *it* (run away, something worse, or maybe even choose to live by my own advice).

My beautiful, brilliant Kya Hazel,

Each moment set before us is a chance to create something good in it. It's easy to pretend like our time is infinite. As you gain years and wisdom, you'll be able to embrace the warm comfort of each moment. It took me a lot of days of freedom, adventure, chasing of passion, lost love, and unrest in my soul to get here. But this morning, I am present to see your smile and hear your giggle. You are learning so fast.

Today, I'm thinking about what legacy will I be able to leave you with? Let me use this opportunity to share my heart and what I know now about how to build your life. I don't want it to take you as many chances as it took me, to get right with God.

You can believe, accept, study, and find comfort in the word of God without fully sanctifying yourself. That's where I got stuck for far too long. To live a life worth existing in, choose to be a child of the one true God, Yahweh. He will bless you endlessly. He will never fail you.

My life to this point has been in part selfish and foolish, and there are real consequences to these actions. You can choose that life—life on your own terms. But you will regret it deeply one day. Each of us must come face-to-face with the Lord one day and reflect on what we made of our collection of moments. *I want yours to be good.*

Let's turn our eyes to where our help comes from. Let's be thankful. Let's see all the joy in our situation. The way the world is made better now because you exist in it, Kya.

Let's choose right. The good and easy path right under our feet. Let's cleanse ourselves to know only love. To exemplify God's goodness in every moment we have left.

Please be an admirer of everything simple and be a *calm* adventurer. Let my story ignite a fire underneath you. That you will use to build a life on solid rock. I don't want you to end with disappointment.

Be love, for that is where you will find joy. There is so much to be said for honesty and kindness, while also valuing yourself. Connection to others and selflessness will save you. Also don't forget how to be silly and have fun. Jesus calls us to share meals with other people with pleasure.

I pray you realize that my mistakes set up your path to be easier somehow.

Each day, wake up and pray. Get ready and take care of your body. It's such an honor to wake up, exercise, shower, and wear a cute outfit. Please never forget that.

Eat home-cooked meals. Take care of your muscles and strength train. Read books and take every chance you can to walk under the sun, whether it's at home or traveling the incredible world. Say yes to building friendships and keeping them too. Go to bed early enough to have quiet time with God over coffee or tea. Give back to those who gave everything they could to you. A phone call can make a day. The mindset of pleasure must be turned on with purpose, every day.

When you are reading this, I don't know who you will be. I just pray God's truth will resonate with you sooner rather than later. Be resilient, be brave. Let the blood of Jesus cover you. Follow Him. This is the good pursuit.

CHAPTER 25

Flashback No. 5

November 2023
(Two months prior to telling the truth)

I sat in the back of the church alone. Dawson begged me to come sit with him and his family at the front. I could not do it.

If I go back in time, and I think about the first time I walked in Dawson's childhood home to meet his parents, I thought, *This is what I want.*

Ultimate love between two individuals exemplifying Jesus. Building a family that laughs together and has fun. Where the kids want to come home and have a cold drink or glass of wine on the weekends when they have grown up and left home. Where Bible studies are hosted twice a week to minister to young folk and to connect with friends. Where the home-cooked meals are overflowing. And the sermons are discussed when you get home from church. With Dawson's father to answer our questions from his deep understanding of the Bible.

I knew I became obsessed with Dawson because I thought he was going to give me *that.* I thought he wanted *that* with me.

And now his one-of-a-kind father was gone, to be in glory.

As I sat in that funeral, I saw the stained-glass reflection on the packed congregation and heard the stories. I saw again the true impact he made on the world.

That was the first time I knew for a fact I could not kill myself. I could not die a terrible person. I had to tell Dawson the truth.

But he just lost his daddy, his hero. I would have to take care of him for a little while until I felt that he was strong enough.

I couldn't wait too long though. This could not wait. I want to be ready to face God any day.

CHAPTER 26

March 28, 2024
Hosanna (Save us.)

The Analise that exists on earth today is not the same woman that wrote this book. I nailed my sin to the cross yesterday at a darkness service, a few days before we celebrate Easter. I'm trying to move on by trusting God *entirely*. Although my heart is healed now, because Dawson did teach me what love looks like, it wasn't enough to make him want to marry me.

I do not deserve sympathy for lying for two years. I just wanted to tell my story as to how I got here, trying to point to my experience of discovering Jesus and rededicating my life to him. This story turned out just like an old Bible story with key takeaway messages. (But still, read the Bible okay.)

Let me try to summarize what's on my heart, from a few different angles.

In the Future

A little girl is supposed to have such a secure and intimate relationship with her daddy that she knows her worth in early adult dating. She's also supposed to see a relationship between her parents that gives her the groundwork on how to value herself and give herself in ultimate love.

As Kya gets older and I do my best to enforce biblical values and a moral compass inside of her and through my relationships around her, I will likely be reminded that each human must walk their own imperfect journey to discovering God, and parents cannot stop a child from their "heroic journey," leading them to return home once again, more enlightened.

But Kya will need to see me act out love, joy, and nurturing in the way God intended a family to operate for her best chance.

I wish I realized this before I had Kya, but we still have *some* time.

In Case You Can Relate at All

If you're a human that has done something bad before, you might agree that you had great advice along the way from both your loved ones and God. You just didn't listen until it was far too late.

But then you realize it's still not too late to start over. The days you have left, you can live within biblical boundaries that will support flourishing.

Most of the women I respect most in this world have encouraged me after my confession, with something like, "We all have our sin, Ana." To which I say, "Most people don't have to do something this bad to get it right." It just brings home the point: sanctify yourself *now* from whatever sin you have.

I do envy the girls who did not waste as much time being ill in relationships as long as I did or picked someone easier or more right for them.

Once, my little cousin at five years old said, "Ana, you sure are pretty but you make bad decisions," as I walked on a dock that had a "No trespassing" sign, which her dad pointed out. We've joked about it ever since. Ugh. Now I have to explain this story to her as she is a young teenager.

Delight Is in the Instruction of Yahweh

I agree with my pastor: something is stirring up in the spiritual realm. The chaos and evil in this world can't go on forever.

Right before I found the guts to confess my sin to Dawson, Pastor Chad began preaching on Revelation, the last book of the Bible. During the same time, the wars between Israel and Gaza flared up and signaled the potential for fulfilling of the last biblical prophecies before Jesus returns.

The loud and clear message from God to our world is, "Now is the time to get our eternal souls right. Repent and follow God." He may have let Satan control this earth for some time, but Jesus holds the seal to this world. One day he will come back for the saints, and he will reign over the earth. So I did what I had to do to face God and *hope* to be called a saint.

I will never be ashamed of the gospel of Jesus Christ. He saved my life.

> Confess your sins to one another and pray for one another, that you may be healed. (James 5:16)

> If only you had paid attention to my commands, your peace would have been like a river, your well-being like the waves of the sea. (Isaiah 48:18)

> The Lord is my shepherd; I shall not want. He makes me lie down in green pastures. He leads me beside still waters. He restores my soul. He leads me in paths of righteousness for his name's sake. (Psalm 23:1–4)

Our Country

To every loving family and human doing life in God's image (whether they realize it and believe in him or not), thank you for being lights in this world.

In a generation where adults stay longer unmarried, I would argue that there are negative effects for all single people. I saw how happy Dawson was with a child—happier than he was single. Having babies, adopting babies, and loving one another fully is something God calls us to do, knowing it's what's best for us. Sure, some people will claim they are happier alone, and I think some people truly are, even though it's not what God wanted originally for them. I think we should keep preaching to young people that independence is not the goal, but healthy adult love with a suitable partner. You'll be happier the sooner you have your own family unit, as God intended it, between a man and a wife.

If a woman knows she wants to be a mother, can our society accept that again? Can that be just as respected as wanting to go to college, grad school, get the career? I can remember wanting to be a mother from when I was like eighteen years old. I think I will tell Kya that both options are just as noble. I never want her to ache for a child like I did, thinking she was too young, when that isn't necessarily a fair argument to tell a woman and man who want to start a family young together. Our country is the one to suffer in this.

For every girl in my position (the hopelessly-in-love part, always feeling inferior in someone else's view of you), if he constantly makes you question, "Why am I not good enough for him?" just remember: you should be focused on your intimate relationship with your father until you're old enough to rely on God as a Father as well. And then one day after you have spent so much time investing in your hobbies and interests, you would be so strong and ready to offer yourself as a potential wife to someone that you have grown to adore *in friendship*. The right one will protect you and pick you as his bride. Be faithful and wait for him. Dream of him and the magic that it will result in. (I was told this part when I was young, and it wasn't enough to control the human instinct to experiment. I wish someone explained the consequences better to me, how I could *ruin* myself.) It will probably take the rest of my life to recover from never hearing Dawson say, "I want to marry you too".

My Healing

While I have shown some symptoms of "losing grips of reality" in in the past, healing has taken over my body. For everyone wondering, the psychologist couldn't deny that I have shown symptoms of borderline personality disorder through my relationship history. While several counselors have deemed it sin rather than true psychosis, you can decide for yourself what you think about me.

My new goals include getting involved at church or in community service, making time for the gym, and sunlight adventures with Kya, plus lots of virtual self-image therapy with my psychologist. I believe that a potential diagnosis in my case can't stand up to the power of Jesus.

I painted my house to make it a new, happy home for Kya. Not that I can really afford it, but now felt like the right time. I'm now like one missed paycheck away from needing to sell my home, but I trust it will be okay. Kya found a loose crayon and scribbled on one white wall almost immediately after the painter left. And it made me laugh rather than cry.

Kya is my everything. She and Sven planted tomatoes earlier this week in the patio planters (that Dawson's mom gave me last summer). Spring has sprung, and the flowers are blooming. I have more time to get to work than ever before with Sven's help now and flexible schedule, taking over some of my babysitting needs.

My prayer for myself each morning is this:

> God, please help me to be grateful and intentional during this season. Turning away from wired responses to new neural pathways filled with the divine consciousness (the Holy Spirit). Help me to talk to you all day, Lord. To remember the Creator of the universe. Give me the energy to properly care for others around me and my earthly body. Please grant strength given the burden of my circumstances. I'm praying that my actions *this year* and all those after will honor your kingdom. It took me twenty-eight years to get here, but here I am.

So What about Dawson?

I received the civil complaint from Dawson to change Kya's last name. I was at work when the certified mail came for a signature, so I had to go wait in line for it at the post office the next morning. I opened it when I went to my car. I could not believe my eyes. Why did it have details stating that I had intentionally slept with a man with similar facial characteristics as Dawson to lie all along? I called him crying, barely able to speak.

"Is this the paperwork that you referred to as being nice to me? I cannot sign this because it is not true," I said.

He told me that they must prove it was fraud for the judge to easily sign off. The complaint was to take Dawson's name off the birth certificate and change Kya's last name. He promised he was not suing me for anything else. And he also promised his goal is to seal the records from the public. I have no idea if one day this legal matter will destroy me or not. But I plan to blindly sign the paperwork and trust him. I told myself I will never hire a lawyer to defend myself in this.

Forgiveness takes one (that's all God calls Dawson to do here). Reconciliation takes two. And maybe that's not what's best for him.

I'm sure some people are relieved that Dawson is exploring his other options for marriage. But as a girl who slept with him recently, I was more devastated and confused in that hotel room in Colorado, once again wishing to die by wondering, *How was that just sex for you?*

God has a funny way of teaching us lessons, huh.

The only thing I have tried to say to Dawson is that I love him and wish to be his honorable wife and suitable partner from here. And I pray that Kya does not lose him. But I respect his free will that he does not feel the same way since he hasn't come home.

He has his own heartbreak in this, and I can't expect anything anymore. I will just continue to be a martyr, screaming from the rooftops how Jesus is our victory in this tragedy, regardless of anything.

It doesn't matter if I end up with more lawsuits. They'll have to drag me kicking and screaming if anyone thinks I belong somewhere other than at home with my baby.

Worthy is the lamb who was slain.

CHAPTER 27

April 8, 2024
(Three months later)

Dawson came over tonight.

I had texted him out of respect that I was seeking some counseling from our pastor (well, at the church he told me that I couldn't attend anymore). That's why I asked if I could still go forward with the planned meeting. I told Dawson that I wanted to talk to the pastor for closure on all that has happened between us *since* I told the truth. As I'd already had so many conversations with wise people about the other part of my sin, this was the part that I still needed help on.

Dawson asked if he could come over to talk with me about the situation first, to make sure I was not misunderstanding his position in this.

I got to show him the new bright-colored paint on my walls. I got to act and speak in a way that honored God. Standing up for myself a few times, but mostly trying to hear him out for my own closure and confidence in my path forward.

We talked and talked. We smiled and laughed some too.

He told me that his brother's wife is pregnant. I am so happy for his family.

We talked about how our sexual relationship hurt me and my therapy.

On his side, he reminded me, "I did choose to marry you, Ana. That was my plan all along. I just wanted more from you. I needed more nurturing from you. Sure, maybe I didn't really deserve it. But I knew something was missing." He said, "What if I decide that I want to go back to that church with you one day?"

I asked about how his dating was going. I did not get any answers there but just a smirk and a certain eye roll.

I joked about how mean it was that he took me off the gym membership. He told me that he would add me back, knowing I can't afford it right now.

He asked me if I had been "intimate" with Sven yet. To which I honestly answered no. He asked if my plan was to marry Sven. To which I was honest again. I wanted (and still want) to marry *him*, but if he didn't want that too, I will find my way to become both a mother *and* a wife, regardless. That would be the best thing for Kya (to be with someone who wants to marry me), given he doesn't come back.

It won't be Sven. I recently learned that he does not believe in the bible or that relationships can ever be happy (he's only interested in being here for Kya).

Dawson told me that I was wrong for reaching out to his family because I wasn't getting the response that I wanted from him. He told me that because I texted his sister about suicide, his family was encouraging him to never talk to me again. I told him that I recognized it was wrong of me to add further chaos into the situation by involving them but that I thought they would understand given the circumstances. I did hold on to some dignity as I told him, I believed that what I am standing up for is right (now).

I took my chance to offer myself to him one last time. I said I would love to be his wife and carry *his* child.

I said, "Don't you think the world is beginning to end too? We have 'seven years' or maybe a little more, if this is the true fulfilling of the prophecy (the ongoing war)."

We kissed and hugged goodbye.

Let me be clear, I want God's will to be done, not mine. But I love *him*.

CHAPTER 28

April 9, 2024
(Three months later)

I had a wild dream last night after going to bed when Dawson left my house.

Dawson was in my home, racing to find Kya.

He found her and stood in front of her.

She was extremely distraught.

She ran into my arms.

The only way I can rationalize this vision is to say that God is telling me to stop waiting and begging Dawson to come home now.

My new life is ahead of me, with Kya as the main character.

APPENDIX A

Recommended Books

These are summary notes from books that I read, as I was trying to learn to love Dawson (while also living in sin). It's only now that I can apply these truths to my own life.

If you find yourself struggling to relate and handle conflict in a romantic relationship, please read these books yourself, not just my quick notes.

1. *How to be an Adult in Relationships* by David Richo
   - "To love alone will not suffice."
   - All of the love in the world can't make a relationship work. It takes skill learned with grace.
   - We feel loved when we receive the following:
     - Attention
     - Acceptance
     - Appreciation
     - Affection
     - Allowing
   - We need these things to live in accord with our own deepest needs and wishes. Jesus offers this to all of us.
   - Intimacy comes only from the joy and wealth of relationship where you are giving and receiving the five *A*s and serving the world/Lord with those skills.
   - *Mindfulness* = Alert witnessing of reality without the following:
     - Judgment
     - Attachment
     - Fear

> ➢ Expectation
> ➢ Defensiveness
> ➢ Bias
> ➢ Control

2. *Created for Connection/ Hold Me Tight* by Kenneth Sanderfer and Sue Johnson
   - You are attached to and dependent on your romantic partner, much in the same way that a child is on a parent, and we are on the Heavenly Father (for nurturing, protection, and soothing). Dependence *can* be healthy.
   - The book is about identifying and expressing underlying emotions with vulnerability and asking the needs to be met in a way that motivates your partner to meet the need rather than be pushed away.
   - Fighting and lashing out is often really because the hurt person is wondering, *Are you there for me? Do I matter to you?* So imagine if instead of getting angry during conflict, you said, "I need you to hold me tight right now, I feel _____."
   - Monogamy resulting in a secure and lasting bond is the ultimate self and sexual fulfillment.
   - The key to the two-way dynamic: Admit the fear. Reach out for reassurance. Partner makes the choice to respond with reassurance. (Jesus is the model of how to love.)
3. *Getting the Love You Want* by Harville Hendrix
   - At some point, you realize your significant other is not perfectly fit and dedicated to mending your unconscious wounds and complicated needs. Negative feelings replace your once romanticized feelings of them. *But* there is true love that can be perfected down to a science. A few tips in doing this are:
     > ➢ See your partner as a unique being, separate from you. They are on their own journey to survive and find joy.
     > ➢ If *you send negativity* to your partner, you are telling them: you are not right doing what you are doing or

being who you are. This is bringing out unconscious desires or wounds in *you*, not necessarily your partner. Explore those feelings with the IMAGO behavior change request dialogues.

> ➤ Eliminate *all* forms of negativity. Negativity is angry, chaotic outbursts but also tone, criticism, frustration, and hurry.
> ➤ Recreate and take caring behaviors seriously. Find out what would really hit the "cared for" button for your partner. Each day, gift them a few types of caring that *they* ask for.

- Caring for your partner saves *you* and heals your own hurt. Humans can only thrive when we have safe, loving relationships.
- The IMAGO dialogue process: When you do _____ (*this*)_____, it makes me feel _____ (*this way*) _____ and I think it's because _____.
- And then your partner would say, "So did I get it right—you feel *this* way? I can see why you feel that way." (This doesn't mean you have to think they are right. But you are respecting and loving them, *trying* to meet their needs.)
- This results in more empathy and more meeting of each other's needs.

APPENDIX B

Shortest Summary Possible
of the Bible in My Eyes

- Delight is in the instruction of Yahweh.
- The Lord God took man and put him in the Garden of Eden to work it and take care of it.
- God gives humans the choice: Partner with him or define good and evil on their own terms (life on their own terms). "Don't eat the fruit for it will surely kill you."
- Abraham and his descendants are given chance after chance, but they end up in exile due to sin.
- A new leader must be sent to transform our hearts and minds.
- *Real power is serving God, serving others, loving the poor, loving your enemy.*
- There will be a future day where all wrongs are made right, and heaven and earth will be united.
- We want the world to be good, but humans wreak havoc time after time.
- We have all sinned, so if God were going to rid the world of sin, he would have to get rid of us. But God is so good that he instead did it without destroying humanity.
- A new King (Jesus) from the line of David gave his life as a ransom for many. His death on the cross covered all the debt that humans owe to God.
- The same power that brought Jesus back to life from the dead can transform us.
- "The Spirit of the Lord Yahweh is upon me because Yahweh has anointed me. To bring good news to the afflicted, He has sent

me to bind up the broken hearted. To proclaim liberty to the captives and freedom to prisoners. To proclaim the favorable year of the Lord and the day of vengeance of our God; to comfort all those who mourn."

- Blessed is the one who delights in the Law of the Lord and who meditates on his law, day and night. He will become like a tree planted by streams of water which gives us fruit in time, and its leaf does not wither, everything he does, he makes it successful.
- This is eternal life that they may know you. The one true God and Jesus whom you have sent.
- Whoever trusts in Him, shall not perish but have eternal life. (We experience eternal life on earth now too, even in the age of death).
- Since you have kept my command to endure patiently, I will also keep you from the hour of trial that is going to come upon the whole world to test those who live on the earth. I am coming soon.

For a deeper dive on the bible, I recommend Jordan Peterson's biblical series. There is no one who can argue with his genius interpretation of how the bible has to be true, and how to apply the teachings to life in this age and how it relates to human consciousness.

APPENDIX C

What Does the Bible Say about Marriage?

- First, you have to understand these dynamics:
  - ➢ The Three in One (God, Jesus and the Holy Spirit)
- Jesus is equal to the Father (God), but he chose to submit to him, and he became our Savior.
  - ➢ The Holy Spirit is equal to the Father and to Jesus, yet it helps us by pointing us to Jesus.
- *Marriage is made to model that kind of love. Jesus, in the nature of God, became a chief "submitter." Wives are to be as the picture of the church submitting to Christ, and husbands are to be like Jesus in giving himself up for her, as Jesus did.*
- *The Lord God said, it is not good for the man to be alone. I will make a suitable helper for him.*
  - ➢ Suitable helper translations = opposite to; complementary.
  - ➢ Advocate, advisor, counsel, comforter, helper, etc.
  - ➢ Companion, equal, friend, no rivalry or competition, inferiority, opposite, lover.
- *"This is bone of my bone and flesh of my flesh… That is why a man leaves his father and mother and is united to his wife, and they become one flesh."*
- *"This is a profound mystery."*